A DAY IN A LIFETIME

by

Alannah Raymond

ISBN 978-0-6151-8312-1

Copyright 2006

All Rights Reserved

Printed in the USA

LuLu.com

DEDICATED TO ALL MY FRIENDS
AND FAMILY WHO SUPPORTED
AND ENCOURAGED ME

Prologue

Alley lives with her mother, in a constant state of pain. Two deaths in her family so close together, Alley's heart had been broken, so many times. It was hard for her show her emotions, except for the few times she actually looked sad.

Alley knew it would take time to mend her broken heart, the fact that Mr. Right could help, only made the anticipation easier to handle.

Where was he? Can she really find happiness in her life?

A DAY IN A LIFETIME

CHAPTER 1

Alley walked into high school with her head held high, trying not to imagine what kind of day she might have.

Jay was his name, the new friend Alley made. She was surprised she remembered; since she was notorious at forgetting names. He was in some of her classes and seemed nice enough, but you never know about anyone.

The day ended before she knew it, grabbing her books she headed for home. Pushing her way through the crowded halls; fresh air finally.

Alley lived close by so she always enjoyed the walk home.

"Hey Alley, need some company?" Jay asked as he caught up to her.

"Sure, I guess," said Alley, not wanting to sound rude.

"How was your day Jay?"

"Ok, it could have been better."

"Yeah, I know what you mean," mumbled Alley.

"Am I bothering you?" Jay asked.

"No, I don't mind; it's just that I have so many friends, nothing personal. I don't mind having you as a friend too."

"It's ok, if you don't want to be friends." Jay said looking genuinely sincere.

"I don't have many friends, we just moved back here a few months before school started. Can we get to know each other?"

"Ok," said Alley smiling.

"You first," Jay said.

"Ok out of curiosity, what do you look for in a girl? Be honest I won't get mad. I'd like to get your opinion."

"What do I look for hmmm, let's see, someone easy to talk too and understand; like wow that's deep. One thing I can't stand is a liar. Not that I think you're lying, because I'm a really good judge of character."

"Oh well don't worry, I am not good at lying anyway. Jay where do you live?"

"A few blocks from you."

"How do you know where I live?"

"Well you were just about to check your mail, right?"

"Oh yea, right, I knew that."

They both looked at each other and giggled.

"So I didn't catch where you moved from," Alley said glancing at her watch to avoid eye contact.

"Columbia, South Carolina," he said smiling.

"I am very attracted to you; are you sure we only met this morning?"

"Uh, as a friend though, right?"

"Well, how do you express your feelings toward someone?"

"Depends on my mood," Jay replied

"Well I just blurt it out, no matter how it sounds. I guess that's one of my downfalls. Sometimes it doesn't even make sense," Alley said.

"Well what if someone asks you how you feel about them?"

"I still say what I feel no matter what. Why are you so curious? Tell the truth, I'm not the judgmental type." Jay asked.

"Well from what I've seen and heard you sound like my dream guy; sweet, generous, fear no option, and easy to talk too. You know what I mean?"

"Wow," he looked flattered.

"What's wrong?"

"Oh nothing really," Jay said grinning.

"That's not fair, I will find it out eventually," said Alley.

"I am so glad I met you, Alley," Jay said laughing.

"Me, too, but it's getting late and I have an appointment."

"Can I walk you to and from school?" Jay asked.

"Sure I'd love that."

"Ok, I'll see you later then, bye Alley."

Alley's eyes sparkled as she said goodbye.

CHAPTER 2

Over the next few weeks Alley's friendship with Jay grew stronger; walking to and from school, and hanging out when time permitted. Months turned into a whole year since Alley had met Jay, with her birthday just around the corner, she sat thinking how wonderful the year had been. Waiting patiently for Jay; remembering the friends made and the fact that Jay seemed to be the best thing in her life now.

"Alley, come here!"

"Huh!" Alley looked up to see Jay coming toward her. Leaping to her feet she ran to him.

"What?"

"I want you to meet someone."

"Oh! Who?"

"She really wants to meet you, we've been friends for about a year, it's time you meet my mom, since I've met yours. Come on lets go," Jay shouted as he ran ahead.

"Wait!" Alley shouted.

"Don't be mean or rude," Jay said seriously as he turned to Alley when they reached the front door.

"What are you saying? Do you really think I would do that?"

"No, sorry come on in."

Jay was the perfect gentlemen, as he opened the door for Alley. "Mom, I'm home, brought someone special for you to meet!" Jay looked at Alley and winked.

"I'm in the kitchen," she yelled back.

4

Walking into the kitchen, Alley didn't know why but she expected to see Jay's dad sitting there; but he told her he had died when he was only eight.

"Hi Alley, I'm Julie. Jay has told me so much about you."

"It's nice to meet you; they weren't bad things were they?" Alley asked.

"No actually, they were wonderful things," she said smiling.

"Uhh...Mom I'll be upstairs on the computer for awhile, Alley you stay and talk to my mom."

"Umm...sure," said Alley.

Julie and Alley were left alone starring at each other, now what?

"Alley, let's go into the living room so we can get to know each other."

Taking a seat at opposite ends of the couch, Alley noticed the many selves of books, a magazine rack, coffee table, television, three sofas including the one they were sitting on, a huge winding staircase that faced the front door and a very large area rug in the center of the room. Alley had never been in a house quite like Jay's.

"So Jay has told me so much about you," Julie began.

"Huh? Oh! What kind of things?" Alley asked suspiciously.

"Well just basics really. You can tell me the rest."

"Let's talk about what Jay has told you first?" Alley begged.

Julie smiled hesitating for a moment. Little did they know Jay stood at the top of the stairs listening.

"What kinds of things has he said?" Alley continued to beg.

"He honors your friendship, loves talking to you, and says he never gets annoyed with you. You're a great listener and you never argue. Sounds like you have a special bond." Julie said.

"Now tell me, how does he feel about me? I mean emotionally that is."

Julie leaned in and whispered, "Just between us he likes you a lot and he is listening to our conversation."

"What?" Alley turned quickly to see Jay coming down the winding staircase.

"Hey, sorry to break this up, but I'm going for a walk, Alley you coming?" Jay stated loudly like he hadn't been listening.

"Sure, Julie it was nice to meet you," Alley stammered as she followed Jay to the door.

"What did she ask you?"

"Basic questions, about me nothing really out of the ordinary. Where are we going?"

"No where in particular, just walking. Alley, you've become one of my best friends. I talk to you more than anyone; it's rare that a guy finds a female they can share feelings with as well as friendship." Jay said.

"It's ok, Jay I hope one day I find a boyfriend that confides and shares his feelings with me as well. I hope to have the close bond that the two of us have. Too many guys just use us and move on." Alley continued.

Jay was silent; he seemed to be recomposing his thoughts. "I totally agree Alley, but just for the record I'm not one of them."

Starring at Jay, Alley thought of how right this guy was for her. A coy smile on her face gave way to deep thoughts, she had to regain her composure when Jay blurted out; "Alley please tell me! What are you think?"

"It's personal," Alley said shyly.

"Come on, we've shared life experiences and personal thoughts up to now." Jay said.

"Us," blurted Alley. It's about us!"

"What about us?" Jay looked puzzled.

"Maybe it's just me, but are we more than just friends?" Alley asked.

Jay stopped, and gazed into her eyes, "Alley would that be such a bad thing? I'm ready, are you?"

"I am too," whispered Alley, now starring at the ground.

"Really, Alley are you ready?"

"Yes Jay, well maybe I am a little afraid."

"What are you afraid of?"

"Of getting hurt, you might get tired of me. What if we aren't meant to be together?" said Alley.

As Alley starred into Jays eyes, she saw sadness, the sparkle had disappeared.

"Do you really think I would get tired of you? You should know me better than that by now."

"Where are we going?" Alley asked changing the subject.

"Walking you home, I guess! I need to be getting back though. I have a lot of things to sort out." Jay turned in the opposite direction and walked away.

"Jay, wait please!" Alley shouted.

"Alley I have to go, not that I am being rude but this discussion can wait till later."

"Ok, I don't like leaving it this way, but maybe it's best for now." She sighed sadly.

As Alley walked quietly through the graveyard I began to reminisce about her past....

Alley had a great relationship with her father until he started taking drugs and drinking heavy. Her mother was a story in itself. Wanting everyone to think she was a victim in all this but, the fighting and the violence, Alley and her sister Taylor knew better.

One thing for sure when their mother was mad watch out!

CHAPTER 3

Alley will never forget the night when her dad came home drunk, all hell broke loose.

Taylor, her sister, and Alley became the target of the abuse. Her mom stepped in and began hitting him to get him to stop. The fight was out of control; suddenly she pulled a gun and shot him.

"Alley and Taylor witnessed the whole thing; afterwards she looked as if she had tears in her eyes."

"Girls you saw nothing, you must not tell anyone. Now run upstairs and stay there." Alley remembered her saying.

From that day forward her mom went day to day pretending nothing ever happened. Taylor and Alley knew different, after all it was very traumatic for a seven year old and an eight year old when it happened. (Taylor was the older one.) That is one night Alley will never forget.

Years passed and Taylor slumped into a deep depression, becoming suicidal with each passing day. Alley seemed to be more worried than her mother about her.

It finally happened five years to the day on the anniversary of her dad's death; Taylor turned thirteen, put a revolver to her head and pulled the trigger. Alley tried to stop her but it was too late. First her dad then Taylor, she keeps telling herself that she has the strength to pull through...

Ring...Ring...; grabbing the phone as she went inside, Alley heard Jay's voice. "Alley, it's Jay, I'll be away for a few weeks,

9

my grandmother is dying. I will call when I return."

Speechless, Alley clung to the phone as she heard the phone click. "My best friend is not going to be around," she whispered. Loneliness was already setting in…

Over the next three weeks, Valentines Day crept up slowly. Not being her favorite day of the year, Alley settled in with a good book. Four chapters in and there was a knock at the door.

Her heart raced when she opened the door to see Jay standing there with open arms. "I missed my best friend," Jay said smiling.

"Missed you too, but why did you pick Valentines Day to come home?"

"To surprise you," Jay said, handing Alley a bouquet of flowers.

"They are beautiful." Alley couldn't control herself; she threw her arms around Jay and kissed him. Jay now felt the passion; he wrapped his strong arms around Alley and kissed her back.

"Alley I have something to ask you," Jay released his grip and took a step back.

"What is it?" Alley asked puzzled.

"Are you ready to take the next step? I tried to ask before I left, but the words wouldn't come out."

"Yes, I'd love too. Curiosity is killing me to find out where this might lead us." Alley replied.

"Really! I thought I was the only one who felt this way."

"Did you bring me anything else?" I mean the flowers are nice, but is there anything else?"

Jay took Alley in his arms and kissed her passionately. "Anymore questions?" Jay asked as I pulled away.

"I miss my sister and my dad" Alley said changing the subject.

"They are in a better place," said Jay reassuring her.

"I wish I could believe that, tomorrow is the anniversary of my sister's death, it's going to be hard for me to get through the day."

Alley grabbed her coat and ran for the door, Jay was close behind. "Follow me there is something you need to see," Alley said sharply.

"What is it Alley? Why are you so upset?"

Alley didn't answer. Thirty minutes later Jay stood beside Alley starring at two graves confused.

"Why are we here?"

"That's my dad and sister," Alley said as she pointed at two headstones side by side.

"Oh sorry I didn't know."

"Now you do," Alley snapped.

Placing his arms around Alley, Jay hoped he could make the pain go away. "I can't imagine your pain, losing two family members so close together."

"Well exactly what happened to your dad?" Alley blurted out.

Jay turned a way. "That's a subject I don't want to talk about."

"Come on, you know my story, tell me yours." She begged.

"This is not the time, nor place, eventually I will, but I'm not ready yet."

"Fine!" Jay knew Alley was upset by the tone in her voice. Alley suggested to head back, but Jay decides to stay awhile. Alley shrugged and walked off leaving him standing there.

CHAPTER 4

All was quiet until Alley topped the stairs. Her mom appeared out of no where; startling her since she was hardly ever at home. "We need to talk," said Alley's mom.

"Since when do we talk? What could you possibly have to say?" Alley screamed, as she rushed by.

"You haven't talked to me since dad's death, you are hardly ever at home and now you want to talk."

"First of all Alley; do you even know what your dad was doing? He was drinking, and doing drugs, among other things. Do you have any idea why I shot him?"

"I stood there speechless.

"That's what I thought; you think I'm just a bad mother; don't you? You think it's my fault your sister committed suicide too."

"Why are you bringing this up today? Tomorrow is the anniversary of Taylor's death. Can't this wait?"

"No we need to talk!"

"Fine! If you'd paid more attention to us, you would have seen the state of depression Taylor was I before she killed herself. Can you even understand my pain? You murdered my father and now my sister is dead too, and it is all because of you."

"I'm sorry; I am not the mothering type. Your father is the

one who wanted children, not me. I never even loved you or Taylor." Glaring at her by this time, covering her ears to drown out the hurtful things she continued to say. She still continued.

"The drugs and drinking, I couldn't take it anymore so I shot him. Guess he did all that because of me."

"What did you do?" She screamed.

"Truth is he found another man in our bed and lost it. I just couldn't let him control my life anymore. Remember when I said pretend I'm not even here? That's because I could careless about you or anything you do."

"I think you are a cruel, twisted witch," Alley screamed at her as she headed for the stairs.

"Don't have any regrets," she yelled back. Alley went to her room turned out the lights and cried herself to sleep with thoughts of suicide filling her head. The next morning she felt the pain of Taylor's death as if it were yesterday. "Taylor would have been sixteen," she whispered. (Alley was fifteen) Quickly dressing she headed for the door; her mother pushed past her without saying a word; climbed into her car and sped away. Alley stood on the front porch breathing in the fresh air as tears welled up in her eyes.

Walking slowly toward the woods, until she reached a huge oak tree, where she sat down to cry. It was then that she heard someone walking and then a voice spoke.

"Are you ok?"

"Yes. What are you doing here Jay?" Alley asked looking up.

"I came to wish you a Happy Birthday. Why are you crying? Please tell me." Jay said sitting down and taking my hand.

"Wait a minute let me catch my breath.."

Placing his strong arms around me, he waited patiently.

'She hates me; my mom hates me."

"What?"

"She told me yesterday that she never cared about Taylor or me; it didn't even bother her when Taylor killed herself or the fact that she shot dad." Jay cupped his hands under Alley's chin so to look into her eyes and reassured her, everything would be ok.

"Jay do you remember when I told you; I thought she was cheating on my dad? I was right, she admitted it. Dad wanted us and she didn't." The tears flowed down her face as she spoke.

"Alley I know how you feel. Can I tell you something?"

"Sure."

"Well, I never told you the whole story about my dad. We were very close, he was my best friend. Dad was on the way home from a business trip, when we got the call. The plane had crashed, there were no survivors. Engine trouble was the reason according to his boss. I went into shock, had a mild heart attack and almost died. I have a bad heart like my dad."

"I'm sorry, I had no idea," said Alley gazing into his eyes.

"It's ok; he died two and a half months before my eighth birthday."

"When is your birthday?"

"February," Jay replied.   14

"Scary, my birthday is today, I turned fifteen," she leaned toward Jay and he embraced her.

"We'd better get back," Jay said taking Alley by the hand.

Days went by as Jay and Alley became closer. Summer was just around the corner, and Alley looked forward to spending it with Jay; until her mother informed her summer camp awaited.

Alley rebelled, she didn't want to go but it seemed she had no choice. They agreed to write everyday. Hoping time would pass by quickly, knowing it was going to be a long summer.

CHAPTER 5

Summer ended none to soon, the first day of school was only a few days away. "I'm sure glad to back in Tennessee," Alley said to herself as the plane landed.

Entering the airport she spotted Jay and Julie waiting for her. Alley wanted to run to Jay but her heavy bags disallowed it. Jay had the biggest smile on his face as Alley threw down her bags and ran to him, wrapping her arms around him and giving him a big kiss.

"How are you Alley?" Julie asked.

"Good and you," I gave Julie a hug too not wanting to be rude.

"Great."

"Now we have to find my other suitcases."

Jay grabbed my bags, and we headed for the baggage claim.

"How was your summer, Jay?"

"Lonely without you; now that your back, don't ever leave me anytime soon, ok."

"I won't, never again, I promise."

"Is that your suitcase?" Julie asked.

"Yes it is thank you."   16

Jay picked up the suitcase and carried it to the truck. It was quite a drive from the airport home to Paris, Tennessee but she was with Jay now and it wouldn't seem that long.

Jay pleaded with Julie when we arrived at my house to let him stay awhile, she agreed and drove away leaving the two of us at the curb.

"Thank god mom's not home," she thought to herself as they went inside.

"You can put the bags over there," Alley said entering her room.

"Let's go for a walk, shall we?" Jay asked.

"Sounds like a plan to me," Alley replied as Jay leaned over and kissed her.

"I missed you Alley, now that your back, I don't know what to do."

"Well you'll think of something, won't you?"

When they reached the top of the stairs Alley spotted her mother, she looked as if she had been drinking.

"Well, well, well, what do we have here?" "Not now mother."

"Yes now, since Jay doesn't know everything about you," she muttered.

"What's that suppose to mean?"

"Your other past, you know what I'm talking about."

"Don't even think about it, you've been drinking," I shouted.

"Jay did you know that Alley is a whore, a drinker and a *****? She uses men to get what she wants, just like her mother. Bet you didn't know that did you?" Alley's mother began to laugh.

17

"No I didn't know," Jay looked at Alley inquisitively.

"I even have pictures to prove it. Be careful Jay, you could get hurt by that evil witch. You're better than her; don't let her get the best of you."

"You just described yourself perfectly," Alley said interrupting.

Alley grabbed Jay by the hand and stormed out of the house.

"What was that all about?" Jay asked.

"Don't tell me you believe her."

"I'm saying I do, but what did she mean by it?"
"She does this every time I get a boyfriend; they fall for it

and their gone. The description is of her and she claims it's me instead of her."

"Oh, I wasn't saying you were any of those things, I am just curious as to why she would say something like that. It doesn't change things between us."

"I hope not. Where are we going?" asked Alley.

"I don't know I was following you."

"Listen, Jay I think we should be getting back, it will be dark soon, mother should be in bed by now and I can deal with her tomorrow."

"Ok, see you tomorrow."

CHAPTER 6

Alley woke the next morning feeling tired, not wanting to deal with her mother. Tired of being called a whore and of all the acquisitions, she decided to put and end to it once and for all. Downstairs she went for a drink of water, only to find her mother in the kitchen.

"Well you are looking pretty rough this morning, my dear daughter. Oh, I'm sorry I forgot your nothing but a little whore. But you don't like the truth do you?"

"Mother you're still drunk! Do you know what I think? You're the whore; you've been sleeping around to get what you want. Just like when dad was alive. You never loved him, you only wanted his…."

"Shut up! You don't know anything!"

"When will you get tired of playing your stupid little games, blaming everything on me, stop denying it you're the whore mother? How many unwanted kids do you have out in this world? Better yet how many diseases do you have? I know for a fact you have AIDS, I saw the doctors report." Speechless she left the room.

"Thank god, silence at last," Alley whispered to herself.

Later that day Alley grabbed a credit card belonging to her mother, which she had used many times and headed for the mall. With school just days away she needed clothes and supplies. It was only a four mile walk and she could use that time to think.

Alley returned with bags of clothes and supplies some where around ten p.m., exhausted she went straight to bed not noticing that Jay had called three times.

Morning came too early as she sorted through the items she bought and put them away. After breakfast she showered and went to see Jay. Julie answered the door only to say Jay was not home and would return later.

"Can you tell him I stopped by? Tell him I'll be home all day."

"Sure, I'll tell him."

Jay caught up with Alley as she walked through the cemetery toward home.

"Alley, wait up! Where were you yesterday?"

"I went shopping; didn't get home until ten p.m. Why?"

"I was looking for you. Why didn't you call me back, I left three messages?"

"I didn't notice you called until this morning."

"Where were you when I stopped by your house?" Alley asked.

"I went to the grocery store for my mother."

"School starts in three days, summer is ending too soon," she said changing the subject.

"I agree Alley, but I can't wait to see what's in store for me this year." Jay chuckled.

"Alley you look like you could use a hug."

20

Alley smiled, wrapped her arms around Jay and whispered, "It has been a stressful week."

"All is calm for now," Jay said.

"Probably not for long, I don't even feel like going home, I am so tired," replied Alley.

"It's ok," Jay said kissing her on the cheek. "Do you mind if I show you something?"

"What is it?"

"Follow me." It took about an hour to reach the cemetery at the other end of town.

"Why are we here?" Alley asked as her chest tightened and her breathing became more rapid. "This is a joke right? I don't need this today."

"Alley, calm down I wanted you to know my father is buried here."

Alley collapsed to the ground, her body limp unable to breath.

Jay quickly ran for help, returning with an ambulance. Hours went by before Jay heard anything about Alley's condition. He was devastated to find out she had taken an over dose of sleeping pills and they had to pump her stomach.

It was unbelievable that she almost died; only a miracle had saved her. Jay was heart broken to think Alley would have done such a thing, but he didn't blame her after the past several days. Jay sat by her bedside until she woke at one a.m. on Saturday briefly, then she slipped back to sleep.

Somewhere around ten a.m. Jay heard Alley calling his name.

"I'm here Alley; how are you?"

"Jay, I'm sorry; I didn't mean to hurt you, it's just that I…"

Unable to finish the sentence she burst into tears.

Jay turned away unable to face her. "I really don't know what to say; I'm just thankful you're…"

"Sorry to interrupt but Alley needs her rest, if she plans on going home in a couple of days, said the duty nurse.

"But she has been sleeping all night!"

"Doctors orders!"

"Ok, fine; get some rest," said Jay as he kissed Alley on the cheek.

Over the next three and a half days Jay was lost without Alley. School had started and she missed two of those days being in the hospital. On Tuesday when Alley was released Jay was there. Alley was waiting outside the hospital when he arrived. "Guess we'll have to walk since you don't have a ride. It will give us a chance to talk."

"Good idea, I think we are long over due on talking." Alley said.

"School started, and I've been busy," Jay began not knowing what to say.

There was a long silence between them. Thirty minutes went by in total silence, when Alley started to run.

"I'll race you," Jay said.

"Ok," shouted Alley running way ahead. Twenty minutes later she slowed down in order for Jay to catch up.

"I give up," said Jay collapsing to the ground. Why did you do it? Why did you try to kill yourself?"

"Well…I…was so stressed from the argument I had with my mother, the pills were convenient; I grabbed the bottle and headed for your house. When your mother told me you weren't home, it stressed me out even more and I took half the bottle before I met up with you. What reason did I have to live?"

Jay was furious with Alley, sensing the fury she sat motionless as he stood before her.

"Why would you think something like that," he said angrily.

"I know you hate your mother, but that is no reason to kill yourself. I know she is hard on you, but seriously, what were you thinking? Jay squatted to gaze deep into Alley's eyes; I know one perfectly good reason why you don't need to kill yourself."

"Why?" Alley asked.

"Me, in case you haven't noticed, I have fallen for you. I am telling the truth, I mean what I said."

Tears filled Alley's eyes as she stood and walked away speechless.

"Alley I wasn't trying to be hard on you, I didn't mean to offend you."

"It's ok, don't be sorry, it's not your fault, you were right about everything; now all I have left is…you. Can you ever forgive me? I didn't mean to hurt you. I'm so very sorry."

"You're forgiven, but if you do anything like this again, I'm not sure what I will do. We should probably be getting home, it's getting late and we have school tomorrow. Your class schedule is at my house, I will give it to you in the morning."

"Thank you," said Alley as Jay hugged her and said goodbye at the door.

They both realized now that there was a beginning for them both. But Alley wasn't out of the water yet, more trouble lied ahead.

CHAPTER 7

On Wednesday Alley returned to school in a great mood, but it ended all too soon with one quick look at her schedule.

There were only a couple of classes she had with Jay. The day turned into longer than usual, when Jay had an appointment that excused him from school early. This meant Alley was all alone; seeing that she was not very popular only left her with one or two friends to spend the rest of the day with.

At the end of the day Alley was walking along when Rose caught up to her. "Hey Alley, wait up!" Rose called out.

"Hey Rose, what's up?"

"Not much. I was wondering if I could walk with you."

"Sure, how have you been?" Alley asked.

"Good, how are you feeling?"

"I feel better now, kind of like my normal self."
"How are things between you and Jay? Be honest."

"Things are good between us, even after the interesting conversation yesterday."

"What was it about?" Rose asked.

"Oh it was about what I did and why? He wanted to know why I tried to kill myself. He told me that I should not have done it. Isn't that weird?"

Before Rose could answer Alley continued. "He said, he

was falling for me too, what ever that's supposed to mean."

"Alley are you blind?"

"No why?"

"He's falling in love with you; I don't think it will be long before he says he loves you. You should honor your friendship and relationship with him. I think the two of you are great together."

"I don't think I could handle a relationship, what if I get hurt."

Alley grew silent; Rose was stunned at what she had said.

"Alley considering how close the two of you are, do you really think he would hurt you?"
"No, but maybe he is lying to me. Do you know any really cute decent guys around here? They are hard to find." Alley replied.

"Really now, Alley, listen to me, think back to the days you've spent together, things he's done and said. He's cute, sensitive, not arrogant or mean. There is chemistry between you, I know for a fact that he likes you."

"I agree, but how do you know he like me? What did he tell you?"

"Jay told me this morning that if anyone ever hurt you they would have to answer to him. He said, he would never forgive himself if anything happened. You broke his heart Alley when you tried to kill yourself. I really think you should give him a chance." Rose waited for Alley to say something.

Alley was silent, inside she knew Rose was right about Jay; she didn't want to hurt him either. She loved his beautiful green eyes, his good looks, and dark brown hair although he was a little on the skinny side. There was no reason not to

25

want him; she had to give him a chance.

"Ok, you win I'll give him a chance." Alley said coyly.

"Great and I will be here for advice that is if you want it from me." Rose replied.

"Well here's my house, Ill talk to you later Alley. Bye"

CHAPTER 8

The next several months went by fast, before Alley knew it, January was here. Jay had gone to France for Christmas break to visit family, leaving her with no one to talk to except Rose.

Alley had other friends but Rose seemed to be easier to talk too about Jay.

Alley walked into school excited at the fact that Jay would be back, only to find him deep in conversation with Rose. They were even kind of secretive all day. Alley wondered what it was all about.

Catching up to Alley after school, Jay asked if he could walk with her since she had been so distant.

"Sure," said Alley. "I thought we walked home together everyday."

"We do or did, but I just wanted to make sure it's still ok, you know." Jay replied.

They walked a ways before the silence broke. "How come you didn't tell me?"

"What?"

"What Rose told you?"

"Oh sorry, I didn't know I was supposed too... What were you and Rose talking about this morning?"

"I asked her why she told you. Is that such a bad thing?" asked Jay.

"At least she was honest and told me how you feel, you couldn't do it." Alley snapped.

"Your wrong I did tell you, I said I was falling for you; isn't that good enough? Or do you need more?"

"Wait that was five months ago. What about now?"

"True, but you're avoiding the question. Do you want it to be more?"

"Yes, I do but…"

"Then what is stopping us?" Jay looked into her eyes; Alley purposely dropped her book bag and reached to pick it up. Jay stopped her, "Alley why do you think I would leave you?"

Alley was shocked to know that Rose had told Jay every single detail about their conversation. She was speechless.

"We can do anything we set our minds too Alley; we can make this work. Follow your heart." Jay waited for her reply.

"You're right," said Alley came through and smiled.

"Good, now how do you feel about us?"

"This…"she wrapped her arms around Jay and kissed him passionately.

Alley stepped back after a few minutes, "I'm falling head over heals in love with you."

"It's about time you were honest with yourself and me."

"I think we should go now it's getting late." Alley said.

   As they walked through the graveyard they kissed goodbye and parted ways. It was getting dark so Alley ran the rest of the way.

CHAPTER 9

Friday came and went before Alley's eyes; she had no homework so Jay went home with her.

Alley's mom was home when they arrived, but they ignored her and went straight to Alley's room.

"You changed your room around. It looks better this way." Jay said looking around.

Alley starred out the window deep in thought, until her mom interrupted. "Alley come here!"

"Jay stay here, I'll be right back." Alley whispered.

"Coming!" Alley yelled back.

"Can I talk to you a minute?" she asked.

"Sure."

"Why is she being so nice?" Alley asked herself.

Alley followed her to the living room and sat down.

"Alley I know I haven't been a very good mother. I want you to know I'm sorry for anything; I've done to you in the past. Can you find it in your heart to forgive me?"

Jay watched from the top of the stairs, he could tell Alley was getting angry.

"What? What are you smoking? You only pretend to be a mother to me, because if you don't they will lock your ass up! I know that your not sorry! No, I will not forgive you after all you've done to me. You've tried to bribe me into doing things, pushed me around, and have been rude to me. You don't love me, never have, and I will not forgive you." Alley shouted.

Storming out of the room, her mother grabbed her hair and threw her into a wall. Put her hands around her throat and tried to choke her. Alley kicked free and ran to the kitchen.

Jay raced down the stairs to the kitchen just in time to see Alley standing there with a butcher knife in hand. "Come any closer mom and I will use it." Alley screamed.

"You wouldn't dare. You know you wouldn't use it."

"The hell I wouldn't!" Alley shoved the knife into her arm.

"Ouch! You little bitch!"

Alley dropped the knife and ran. Half way up the stairs her mother caught her knife in hand and stuck it deep into Alley's leg. Loosing her balance Alley tumbled a quarter of the way down the stairs. Her mom ripped the knife out of her leg, Jay reached her just in time before she jammed it into Alley's ribs. Grabbing the knife from her hand, he threw it half way across the room, and pushed her off Alley.

Terrified she grabbed her keys, ran to her car and drove away. "Are you alright, Alley?"

"Yes Jay my leg hurts but I'm fine." Jay helped her up, but she only walked a few feet before she collapsed. The paramedics were there in about ten minutes, and Alley was taken to the hospital with Jay close by her side.

Alley woke up the next morning to find Jay asleep, head resting on her bed. "Jay are you awake?" she whispered.

"Yes, I'm am sweetie, how are you feeling?"

"Horrible, my leg hurts like crazy."

"I wanted to kill your mother yesterday, but I knew if I did we wouldn't be together. I couldn't bear being without you."

"Same here," said Alley smiling.

"Alley I called the police, they are going to lock her up for awhile. You can still stay at the house. Are you mad at me for it?"

"No actually, oww! Glad you did."

"Are you alright?"

"Yeah I'll be okay, just a sudden pain that's all."

Jay called the nurse to give her something for pain, and settled in so she could get some rest.

Sunday evening came too quickly; Jay had to leave in order to go to school on Monday.

"Bye Jay," Alley said softly as he left the room.

A week went bye before she was released, but she had to wear a cast for two weeks after. It would come off just before her birthday.

CHAPTER 10

The school year was over before Alley knew it and summer was around the corner. This year Alley could finally spend it with Jay. Alley said goodbye to her friends at the end of the day and headed home.

"Wait up, Alley," Jay yelled, "I have some news. My mom wants to know if you'd like to go to Miami with us. We will be gone all summer. Do you want to go?"

"I'd love too, but my mom gets out of jail in June she may try to get me."

"We'll be long gone by then, we're flying, and your ticket is already paid for. I kind of figured you would say yes."

"Jay I could have paid for my own ticket, you didn't have too."

"I wanted too Alley, trust me you don't need to worry about anything. Oh and one other thing, this is really important so pay attention, I don't regret any time we've spent together. I truly cherish you; even though your mother has gotten on my last nerve, I have completely fallen in love with you."

"I love you too with all my heart." Alley whispered.

Julie was in the kitchen when they told her the news of Alley going to Miami. "Mom," whispered Jay, I told her how I feel.

Julie smiled, "Alley we are leaving around eleven a.m. Saturday. Will that be enough time to pack?"

"Yes, it will be great, thank you."

"Mom I'm going to walk Alley home, I will be back soon."

"Ok, be back for dinner."

"Bye Julie and thanks again for inviting me."

Jay stayed awhile at Alley's before heading back.

   Night fall came and Alley could hardly sleep thinking of the wonderful time she would have with Jay in Miami.

Alley was packed and ready to go, but no word from Jay or Julie until about ten thirty. Thirty minutes early, made no difference because she had packed the night before and was ready. The ride to the airport was quiet as we watched the scenery fly by.

One forty five, the plane was right on time, Alley settled in for the flight to Miami as she reminisced abut the past and knew it was the beginning of good things to come.

CHAPTER 11

"All went well over the summer, long romantic walks on the beach, great tanning, hours of shopping, and did I mention the romantic walks with Jay."

"Oh Alley, I am so glad you and Jay had such a wonderful time, did anything interesting happen?" Rose asked.

"What do you mean?"

"You know what I mean." She giggled.

"No I wouldn't do something like that, I'm not like my mother," Alley stated truthfully.

"Where's Jay, he's going to be late," said Alley.

Alley and Rose headed to class; she knew it was going to be a long day. Jay was scarce most of the day, leaving Alley to wonder what was going on.

After school Jay caught up to Alley but he wasn't alone, some of his friends were tagging along.

"Hey guys, what are we doing?" Alley asked.

"Well, Alley today is Friday and it is time for fun," replied Jay with a suspicious smile.

"Where is this so called fun?" Alley asked.

"Oh, you'll see."

Alley had no idea what she was in for, all she knew was, she trusted Jay completely.

Following close behind, Alley was lead to a big park where music was blasting, and there was lots of food and drink.

"A party, what is the occasion?" Alley asked.

"It's a school party," Rose exclaimed.

"Why is the music is all rock?"

"That's what we requested, everyone here likes rock music."

Alley just couldn't get into the dancing mood, she stood watching the others so intensely she had no idea Jay was behind her.

"Alley, Alley!" She heard someone shout.

"What?"

"Don't you even recognize your own boyfriend?"
"Oh sorry, I didn't know it was you."

"It's okay; I was just messing with you. Guess what Alley? Guess what our buddy Gerald did."

"Do I even want to know?"

"Gerald poured liquor in the drinks. At least I think he did."

"Okay."

"I'll be back in a minute." Jay said.

Alley waited for a while and Jay did not return, she decided to go and see Rose. Finding her dancing with a few others, she decided to join them. H.I.M. blared out the song, *Riding in These Arms*, which was Alley's favorite song.

"Alley!" Jay shouted over the music. She did not hear him, so he decided to go out and get her; before he reached the dance area his friend Gerald pulled him aside.

Alley was still dancing an hour later. When he finally returned at eleven forty five p.m.; he spotted Alley, Rose and few others dancing. He stood there laughing to himself. Fifteen minutes later a slow song played and for some strange reason he had the urge to dance. Even it was not his favorite thing to do. He looked around for Alley she was no where in sight. No one seemed to know where she was.

"Guess who?"

"Where were you?" Jay said turning around.

"Getting some punch, why?"

"Alley how many cups of punch have you had?"

"One."

"Okay, good since you're here will you dance with me?"

"You already know my answer silly, yes of course."

Taking my hand he led me to the dance area, wrapped his arms around my waist and we dance for ten minutes with my head on his shoulder.

"It's getting later Alley, maybe we should be getting home."

"I don't want this night to end," Alley said reluctantly, but she followed.

There was an unusual silence between them all the way home. When they reach the house Jay kissed Alley good night and left her stand there on the porch. Alley watched until he was out of sight, went upstairs and straight to bed.

CHAPTER 12

Storms rolled in over the next few days which made the days miserable. Jay was busy so he hadn't been over to visit. His mom had a list of things around the house for him to do and that was taking up all of his time.

Later that day while Jay and Julie were in town he looked for a special present for Alley, he thought she deserved it since after all she made his life complete.

Alley slept all weekend for lack of anything better to do. Jay surprised on Sunday evening even though the rain was still pouring down. Finding the door unlocked Jay let himself in, and went straight upstairs to Alley's room.

Jay found her sleeping, so he lay down beside her, starring at the back of her head. Alley rolled over seconds later and opened her eyes.

"Good evening love," Jay said smiling.

"Hello, what are you doing here?"

"Haven't you ever heard of just stopping by?"

"Yes, but haven't you ever heard of beauty sleep?"

"Yes but I haven't seen you all weekend, I never would have guessed you would be sleeping."

"Oh thanks. Alley said with a sigh. I can't help it rain makes me sleepy. I'm glad it rained, I feel better than ever, all energized and refreshed," she said smiling.

Sitting up back against the wall, "tell me something Jay, why are you so nice to me. How come you treat me so special, I'm just a regular person."

"You deserve it Alley, plus I have never been the mean type. I guess you could say; I was born this way. I love you like crazy, your beautiful, smart, fun, quiet at times, honest, loving, caring, outgoing, down to earth and last but not least you're my girlfriend and your not leaving me anytime soon if I can help it." Jay laughed leaning in to kiss me.

Realizing it was five o'clock, Jay knew he had to leave

Even though he didn't want too, so he said his goodbye

and left.

"Bye, my beauty."

"Bye, love you."

"Love you too. Bye" Jay said as he walked away.

CHAPTER 13

The first full day of school was wonderful. Alley spent time with all her friends. At the end of the day Jay told Alley he was going over to a friend's house that he needed to talk to him about something important.

Alley ended up walking home with Carly and Rose.

"Alley wait up," they shouted.

"Oh, hey guys, what's up?"

"Guess what I heard?" Carly asked.

"Jay's in love with you," both Carly and Rose blurted out.

"Ummm… I already know that."

"No Alley you know he loves you, but not what you mean to him."

"Oh really, did he tell you?"
 "Now that would be something you would have to ask him." Rose replied.

"Oh, come on, you guys have been great at telling what Jay says."

"Well hey, he's your man not ours." Carly said.

"Listen, we have to go, right Rose."

"Right we have to go over to Gerald's house; at least we think that's where Jay is. He said Gerald had to show him something. We will let you know what it is ok." Rose replied.

   The next couple of days went by fast and she didn't recall Rose or Carly telling her what happened at Gerald's. It was now Friday, so after school; she cornered Carly and Rose to find out.

"You will find out tonight. That's all we can say."

Jay caught up to her on the way home. "Alley what are you doing?"

"Not much why do you ask?"

"Cause I was wondering if I can steal you away for awhile?"

"I don't see why not. Where are we going?"

"Well actually I have something for you."

"Really? I don't need anything. You're all I need."

"I know but can I show you?" Jay pulled out the most beautiful diamond heart necklace with the inscription Alley and Jay. I didn't know what to say. "It's beautiful," Alley stammered.

"I had it made especially for you and it didn't cost a fortune; thankfully my mom has a friend who makes this kind of thing."

"Cool, but it's not my birthday, what's the occasion?"

"It's just that I felt like doing, something special for you."

"Can I put it on you?"

"Oh yes of course," Alley turn and pulled her hair up.

"It's so beautiful on you." Jay said smiling.

40

"Thank you," said Alley giving Jay a big hug and kiss.

"Your welcome, would you like to go for a walk?"

"Sure."

After walking for what seemed like forever, Jay finally asked; "Has your mother done anything strange to you lately?"

"No, but don't jinx me."

"Now what makes you think I would want to do that?"

"I have no clue," Alley said smiling

Jay took her into his arms and kissed her for several minutes afterwards, she invited him over to her house and he graciously accepted.

CHAPTER 14

It took thirty minutes to get to Alley's house, quickly glancing around she didn't see her mother's car. She was relieved.

Everything seemed normal when they went inside, but they both had a gut feeling it wasn't. As soon as they reached the top of the stairs, a car pulled into the driveway. Quickly they ran to Alley's room, a glance out the window told them she was not alone. "I know that man, he is very familiar, oh my god, I don't believe it! That witch, Jay we can't let her know we are here."

"Why?" He looked confused.

"She's brought someone home with her."
 "Ok," he said looking somewhat like he understood.

Before another word was spoken the front door flew open...
"I had a wonderful time, Tom thank you."

"Me too." He replied.

"Do you want to stay for a drink?"

"Actually, is Alley here?"
  Jay looked at Alley.

"Umm, let me check," she said looking toward the stairs.

"Alley, come down here please, I know your up there!"

"We're busted, Jay stay here please."

He insisted he go along, being worried about what might happen, but he agreed to stay put.

Alley walked down the stairs very slowly.

"Hey Alley, long time no see!"

"That voice," Alley thought to herself, "I know that voice." Then it hit her.

"Don't you remember your old uncle?" She was right it was her dad's brother. By the look in her mom's eyes she wasn't ready to play nice.

"Alley, it's time you knew the truth."

Alley's mom stared at him in shock

"Why now, Tom?"

"Trust me," he replied.

Worry was setting in, but Alley showed no remorse.

"Alley let's go into the living room shall we?"

   Following not wanting to make things worse, she noticed that Jay was close behind in the hall.

"Alley by now you're wondering what this is all about, am I right?" Uncle Tom asked. First off let's start with your father, he was a smart man, but I am sure you are aware he was running around on your mother. Your mother caught him red handed in bed with her sister. That's when he started drinking.

Of course at the same time your mother was sleeping with me.

There was this one time when he left and I slipped in, Taylor and you came home and I had to hide. That was the night she shot your dad. You girls were just plain stupid and stood there

43

and watched. The two of you were sent to your rooms and I left before the cops got here. Furthermore, do you know why your sister killed herself?"

"Dad," I stammered.

"No it was because of me, I was raping her over and over again. Then three years later, bang, bang she's dead."

Alley burst into tears, "mother!" She shouted, "Why didn't you do anything?" Turning to run Tom grabbed her arm and pulled her close.

"If she'd told, I would have killed her." Tom said harshly. "If you know what's good for you, you'll keep your mouth shut too."

Tom dragged her back into the living room; where her mom stood holding a butcher knife behind her back.

Suddenly Tom grabbed her and pulled her tighter to his body, kissing her neck and feeling her in places she wanted nothing to do with. Alley tried to get out of his grasp, freeing from his clutches with her shirt half torn off. Tom grabbed her leg and Alley fell with a thud. Jay had heard and walked downstairs.

"Mom!" Alley screamed. "You can use that knife anytime now."

Mom finally lashed out and stabbed Tom in the chest.

He shot a cold look as he fell to the floor.

"What happened?" Jay asked when he reached Alley.

"He tried to rape me, I got away."

"Are you ok?"

"I'm fine, hurt pride and a torn shirt is all."

"Thank god." Jay whispered.

"Alley are you ok," Alley turned and ran to her.

44

"You saved my life! But why did you do it?"

"Just for the record, I don't exactly love you, but I don't hate you either. I also did it to get him out of my life. Now I have to put him somewhere. I'll take him to the dump."

Alley took a step back. Her mother took Tom by his feet drug him to the car, placed him in the trunk and drove away.

Jay wanted to hold Alley and tell her everything would be alright, but he knew it would take more than that to make the pain go away.

"Alley are you ok?"

"I'm glad you're here." Alley replied, giving him a hug.

"If I'd known what he was up to I'd have been there in a flash to help you. I'm sorry."

Cupping Jay's face in her hands, she told him it was not his fault. "I feel safe when you're around. There is no way anyone could have known that was going to happen."

"I'm glad you feel that way," Jay replied giving her a kiss.

"Maybe you should put on a shirt now."

"That can wait; I just want you to hold me."

Alley walked away and spotted a pile of pictures on the floor. Bending down to pick them up she noticed they were of her dad, mom, Taylor, and herself. One stood out from the rest, it was dated 2/14, the day of Taylor's death. It was a picture of Tom handing Taylor a gun.

"Oh my god, he wasn't lying! That sick bastard!" Alley screamed.

"What is it?" Jay asked as he saw the picture.

"Oh god, your right!"

45

Wishing that he could take away all the pain she was feeling, more than ever now, Jay hugged her.

He didn't want to leave Alley alone; her mother probably wouldn't be home before morning, so he called his mom to say he was staying at Alley's for the night.

Alley went to her room to lie down and Jay followed. As she lay looking up at the ceiling, she was trying to sort out the events of what had just happened. It was hard to believe that her uncle would have tried such a thing.

Jay curled up beside her, tried to figure out how one person could go through what she had and still be strong.

"Alley you're a strong person, all that you've been through, that's one of the reason I love you. I wouldn't have the strength to go through it myself with my heart problems, well actually heart disease and all, it would have been way to much for me."

Alley was speechless as he lay next to her.

"I wish I didn't have to worry about dying because of this disease, but I have too." Jay turned away from Alley as she faced him.

"When I'm with you, nothing else matters Alley. I'm happy I met you."

"Me too," Alley said smiling. "I don't think I would have made it without you. I will always love you with all my heart…"The n she drifted off to sleep.

"Sweet dreams love," he said as he gently kissed her cheek.

CHAPTER 15

Alley woke the next morning feeling refreshed with Jay by her side. She watched as he slept thinking about how wonderful he was and how safe she felt.

"He's so cute and peaceful," she thought to herself.

After a few minutes Jay opened his eyes to find Alley cuddled next to him with a big smile on her face.

"Good morning beautiful."

"Good morning," she said cuddling closer.

"I love you so much," Jay whispered.

"It's like heaven laying her next to you." Alley whispered as Jay flashed a smile

"We'd better get up," Jay said as he walked to the window.

"It looks like it's going to rain."

"I'll walk you home, give me a minute to get dressed," Alley said.

As they walked through the woods, Alley thanked Jay for not leaving her alone last night.

"No problem, I'd do anything for you Alley."

The walk to Jay's was faster than expected, Alley kissed Jay goodbye at the door.

Alley took the route through the cemetery and stopped at Taylor's and her dad's graves. Sitting down between the two, she began to ask Taylor why she hadn't told her about the day she shot herself.

"If I'd only know Taylor, maybe I could have helped. Why did the two of you leave me all alone? I love and miss you both so much." Hours later it was too much Alley had to leave. She said her goodbyes and walked home.

The next day at school seemed longer than usual and very boring. Months drug by and her birthday rolled in before she knew it. She was at home reading when a knock on the door interrupted her. Knowing it was Jay she raced to the door and found only a note. It read: "Look outside."

Puzzled she went to the window, a midnight blue Volkswagen convertible was parked in the driveway. She raced downstairs to find a note on the windshield, "Alley what I could never have. Don't get too happy, it's still going to be the same around here. –Mom."

Alley was shocked, what on earth possessed her to buy a car, especially for her? Immediately she went to her mom's room to say thank you at least, but she was gone.

Jay stopped by while Alley was sitting in the car.

"Wow! Whose beautiful baby is this?" Jay exclaimed.

"You wouldn't believe me if I told you."

"Try me."

"Mother gave it to me, I'm not sure why."

"Well be happy, you at least have your own car."

"I am trust me," she said smiling.

"Nice," he said leaning in the window."

"Happy Birthday Alley," Jay said giving her a kiss.

"Where's my present?"

"You're looking at him."

"Are you mine forever?" I asked coyly.

"Duh!" They both laughed.

"Just making sure because, I'll never let you go."

"Same here, babe."

"Jay you saved my life, I would be dead by now if you hadn't been around."

"It was my pleasure, we've been through a lot together, and I wouldn't trade any of it for the world."

"I love you with every inch of my heart and soul," Alley replied.

Suddenly she felt as if she was going to pass out.

"Are you ok?"

"I think so I lost my breath, there for a few seconds."

"Was what I said too much?"

"It's just that you have made me love you even more. I never thought I could love someone so much. I'd give up everything for you."

"You've already got me babe and that's forever."

Alley could tell he meant every word of it as she looked at him and smiled. Jay gave her a big hug as she got out of the car.

"Alley I never thought we would end up like this. But I'm glad we did."

"Ok keep going tell me more." Alley said flashing him a smile.

"When I first met you, I actually felt a connection between us as friends. Then after I got to know you, you seemed like my perfect dream girl. Your past gave way to me feeling sorry for you, not wanting you to have more pain in your life. My heart went out to you as we became closer; truth is I've loved you for a long time, since I first laid eyes on you."

"I know what you mean; I never thought I could love someone as much as I love you. But I'm glad we met, you're the only reason I am still living."

"I'm glad you finally understand Alley. If it weren't for everything that has happened I don't think we would be here right now. Maybe what they say is true, everything happens for a reason."

Alley was speechless, Jay starred at her trying to figure out what she was thinking. Finally she smiled and gave him a hug. "I love you with all my heart."

"I love you too Alley and I always will."

They knew they had bonded in a way like no other.

CHAPTER 16

Fall break was just a few days away, when Jay jumped into his new car and headed for Alley's. He stopped along the way to pick up a special gift for their anniversary.

Alley met him at the door when she heard a car pull up; she stood astonished when she saw the red corvette.

"Do you like it?"

"Yes, I do it's nice."

Jay looked a little different today than he had before. She couldn't quite put her finger on it at first. Then it came to her. He was becoming a man.

Alley listened as Jay explained the features of the car and how excited he was to have it. "Congratulations!" Alley said smiling.

"Thank you, I love you Alley but I'd better be going." Jay said winking at her.

"I love you too, take care." Alley said as Jay drove away.

Alley went back to her cleaning and then to bed early.

Moments later Jay, as the light turned green, a truck ran a red light smashing into Jay's car. It hit so hard the car spun around in the road and flipped. Jay was left unconscious, but still breathing...

Julie was called to the hospital and told they weren't sure if he would make or not, his heart was getting weaker.

Doctors said it was a miracle he even survived the crash.

Turns out the driver of the truck was drunk.

"Is there anything I can do?" Julie asked.

"I'm sorry, it's just a matter of time," replied the doctor.

He left the room so Julie could be alone with Jay. A nurse came in to check his monitors. Jay opened his eyes and tried to speak. "You need to save your energy, try not to talk," said the nurse.

"Mom, please call Alley for me, she needs to know."

Jay fell back into an unconscious state.

"Ok I will call her."

Alley was sitting on the couch when the phone rang. "Alley it's Julie, umm... I don't know how to tell you this but..."

"Jay's ok isn't he, he's not leaving me or anything," She panicked.

"No it's not that, he's in the hospital."

"Is he alright? Is he alive?" Tears were now streaming down my face.

"Alley, he's in critical condition, he could die."

"Oh god, Julie can I come see him please."

"Yes Alley, see you soon." The phone went dead.

Silently Alley stood wondering whether or not Jay was going to make it, all she could do was pray now...

52

"Snap out of it," she told herself and ran down the stairs and told her mom where she was going, and then she headed towards the hospital. She answered with an "Okay" and went into the kitchen.

Alley asked a nurse which room Jay was in, when Julie appeared and lead her to him. Room 237 she will never forget that number…

Holding back the tears was hard, as Julie gave them time alone.

It wasn't going to be easy pretending everything would be ok.

Jay was asleep or at least appeared to be, he was covered in bandages the entire length of his body. Alley pulled up a chair and sat next to him. The way he looked was too much to bear so she started to cry.

"Alley, is that you why are you crying?" Jay asked.

Alley was unable to look at him. He tried to move, but couldn't.

"I'm alright Alley," he whispered.

Finally she wound the words to say. "No your no otherwise you would be sitting next to me with your arms wrapped around me."

"I'm lying next to you isn't that enough, even though the bandages are in the way. I feel your pain, stop worrying."

"I'll try," She said calmly and leaned over and kissed his bandaged head.

"Get some rest, I love you, I will come back tomorrow."
"I love you too, I always will. See you later."

Jay was smiling when she left the room, or tried to anyways…

What would the next few days bring? Nothing would ever be the same again…

CHAPTER 17

Julie met her in the hall, and explained what had happened to Jay. She said he was lucky to be alive, and to be grateful for what the doctors were doing even if he didn't have much time left.

"How long does he have?"

"Maybe a few weeks at most; spending time with him now is more precious to me than anything else."

"What can I do Julie?'

"Spend as much time with him as possible, that way he remains content through all of this."

"Doesn't he know?" I was devastated to find that out.

"No, he doesn't and it is better that way for now, over the next few days I will let you tell him that if you don't mind. I think it would be better coming from you."

"I will take care of it, but for now I need to go," Alley said brushing past Julie and out of the hospital...

Reaching the front door, fresh air hit her in the face. The tears began to stream down Alley's cheeks. She never felt that anyone truly loved her until now.

The walk home seemed lonely, cutting through the woods made it even longer but Alley decided to stop at the cemetery on her way home. She looked around and saw a couple of freshly dug graves, and wondered who they were for.

A quick look at her watch revealed five thirty almost dark and still a ways to go. The afternoon had passed by quickly and the storm clouds were rolling in. It was beginning to sprinkle so Alley started to run.

By the time she reached the house she was soaked and it was pouring rain, the thunder roared and the lightning cracked.

Drenched from head to toe, she rummaged through her closet for something to wear. Finding a multicolored jumpsuit in shades of purple with a few others mixed in, she quickly changed and settled in to watch the storm.

The thundered roared over head, her stomach was almost as loud, so she headed down to the kitchen for something to eat.

Minutes later her stomach had quieted down, which is more than she could say for the thunder. She curled up in her warm bed and drifted off to sleep.

Alley awoke the next morning terrified. The weird dream that had filled her head was that she was diagnosed with cancer. She had no idea where the dream came from but it definitely wasn't something Alley wanted to be true...

Hurrying off to the hospital to see Jay, I had to tell him of my dream. Dreading the fact I had to tell him of his dying, "maybe I shouldn't tell him just yet; no I promised Julie I would, but it was going to be hard." In the dream she found out that she had cancer, with no visible signs, and that she died an hour after Jay's funeral...

He was buried on Wednesday. Seems strange though; today is Tuesday. Jay was buried behind her house in the cemetery,

She awoke and was relieved. Could this be some kind of omen?

Why would she have strange dreams all of a sudden? Is it a sign to tell Alley something? She found it rather awkward to see herself dying. It's pretty weird.

It would be very lonely when Jay is gone, and there will be no reason for her to live. The ride to the hospital was very long, all these crazy ideas running through her head, what if she really did have cancer? What then?

At the hospital Alley decided to make an appointment just to be on the safe side. What if, she kept asking herself? It just so happened that an appointment was available, so Alley was taken to a room and prepared for an examination. One hour later she was awakened by a nurse for the results...

"Is it good news?"

"Sorry the news isn't good," the nurse replied.

"My worst fears had come true, what is the bad news?"

"You have leukemia, it's moving rapidly. The doctors are puzzled though, you have no signs. It seems you may only have a few weeks to live. It's time to make the best of the last days you have."

"What about treatment, is there anything they can do?"

"It's too late for treatment it's in the final stages. Your immune system is way too weak, I'm sorry."

Devastated over what she just heard, Alley went to visit Jay and tell him what Alley promised and that she too was dying...

"Jay are you awake?"

"Yes, silly what's wrong?"

56

"It seems the past couple of days have been filled with
nothing but bad news," She tried to hold back the tears.

"What are you talking about, what bad news?" Jay asked.

"I have leukemia, it's too late for treatment, and I'm dying Jay.
My immune system is weak and getting weaker as we speak.
What's even worse is I have to tell you, that you're dying too,
you don't have much time left either."

"Alley don't cry, look at the bright side when I die I won't be
covered in all these bandages." Jay laughed. She kind of
laughed too.

"I've enjoyed our time together and we can still be together,
it's worth dying for."

Alley turned away unable to hold back the tears.

"Jay, how do you always know the right words to say?"

"Because I say what I feel, and what I feel is more love for you
than ever before. You could look at me Alley."

"I can't."

"Please?" He begged.

Turning slowly, she faced Jay, in total silence as he continued.

"We've been happy together and we've felt pain together; now
it's time to let go of the pain and go peacefully. No more pain
or sorrow, just a better place."

"But I don't want us to die; I want us to live our lives until we
are eighty."

"I want to live too Alley but not like this, no casts or crutches,
or without limbs. I would want it like before the accident. We
are going to die and there isn't any thing we can do about it.
Now come here and give me a hug."

57

She came and hugged him. "You'd better go and let me rest, just remember I will love you forever and always."

"You stole my words." Alley laughed.

"I love you Jay."

"I love you too. Bye."

CHAPTER 19

Alley ran into Julie talking to a doctor down the hall.
Julie was very compassionate when she heard the news of
Alley's leukemia. She tried to console her, and asked if Jay
knew. Alley explained there was no time left for treatment
and it was only a matter of weeks. The fact Jay took it so well
was hard to believe. But he was right it was better than living
in a hospital bed the rest his life.

"Can I ask you something, Julie?"

"Sure Alley what is it?"

"I have one request, I'd like for you to do for me. Would
it be possible for Jay and I to be buried side by side?"

She pondered over it for a few minutes, before she answered,
but her request was granted.

"Thank you Julie, it means so much to me. I'd better be
going now, I'll come back tomorrow."

She raced home before the rain hit, the storms didn't seem
to be over yet. Steeping out of the shower the phone
was ringing, so Alley ran to get it.

It was Julie saying that Jay had died an hour after she left. Funeral arrangements had been set for twelve p.m. tomorrow at the chapel across from the cemetery, with burial at two p.m.

"It's only Wednesday" She said out loud, "Why so soon?"

She crawled into bed and cried herself to sleep.

She awoke the next day feeling weaker than Tuesday. It was eleven twenty five and Alley had to hurry. She found the only black dress she had and it looked like a strapless prom gown, but it would have to do. She grabbed her coat and headed out the door. Alley thought walking would be better. So she left the car parked in the driveway.

Arriving sharply at twelve, she ran to Julie and gave her a big hug. She led her to the casket where Jay laid so peaceful.

"He is still as handsome as he ever was." Julie whispered, "He's in a better place now and you can be with him soon." They both smiled at that very moment, because they both knew that Alley would be with Jay forever.

As the day went on, it became more of a blur, by one forty five they took Jay for his final ride. They placed him in a beautiful black limousine and drove him to the cemetery. Alley followed behind on foot. The funeral was beautiful; she couldn't have been more pleased. Julie and Alley stayed behind afterwards for their goodbyes. Alley said that she would be joining him soon. She kneeled down placing a white rose on his casket and told him she loved him. Then she stood up and left…

As Alley walked home she became weaker with each step she took. Finally she collapsed to the ground and there she lay, until a friend came along and called 911. The ambulance arrived but it was too late. Alley's funeral was as beautiful as Jay's.

Friends and relatives came to say their last goodbyes.

They all knew Alley had only one wish in life, and it was granted that very day.

Alley and Jay would be together forever and that love goes forever. Not even death can stop it.

This book is written by a teenager, who looks at the reality of life. Everyday experiences and the devastation that haunts us each day. Knowing that life experiences torment us and break our hearts. But she seems to find good in everyone. Letting her imagination run wild in this world of pain and suffering, not knowing what each day will bring.

She wrote this book with feelings from the heart.